LIBRARY MOUSE

D0247658

DANIEL KIRK

Abrams Books for Young Readers
New York

For my friends at the Glen Ridge Library, the kids at Glen Acres School, and all the librarians and teachers whose joy it is to help us discover a world of imagination through reading and writing.
—D. K.

The Library of Congress has catalogued the original edition of this book as follows:

Kirk, Daniel.
Library mouse / Daniel Kirk.
p. cm.
Summary: Sam, a shy but creative mouse who lives in a library, decides to write and illustrate his own stories which he places on the shelves with the other library books but when children find the tales, they all want to meet the author.

[1. Authorship—Fiction. 2. Libraries—Fiction. 3. Mice—Fiction.] I. Title.
PZ7.K6339Lib 2007
[E]—dc22
2006031851

ISBN 978-0-8109-9346-4

Paperback ISBN 978-0-8109-8929-0

Text and illustrations copyright © 2007 Daniel Kirk

Book design by Chad W. Beckerman

Originally published in 2007 by Abrams Books for Young Readers, an imprint of ABRAMS. This edition published in 2009. All rights reserved. No portion of this book may be reproduced, stored in a retrieval system, or transmitted in any form or by any means, mechanical, electronic, photocopying, recording, or otherwise, without written permission from the publisher.

Printed and bound in China
10 9 8 7 6 5 4 3 2 1

Abrams Books for Young Readers are available at special discounts when purchased in quantity for premiums and promotions as well as fundraising or educational use. Special editions can also be created to specification. For details, contact specialmarkets@abramsbooks.com or the address below.

ABRAMS
THE ART OF BOOKS SINCE 1949
72-82 Rosebery Avenue
London
EC1R 4RW
www.abramsbooks.co.uk

SAM WAS A LIBRARY MOUSE. His home was in a little hole in the wall behind the children's reference books, and he thought that life was very good indeed.

FICTION
I ♥ BOOKS
FICTION
READ!
BIOGRAPHY

Every day, when the library was full of people walking up and down the aisles, studying, checking out books, and working on the computers, Sam was curled up in his little hole, sound asleep. Every night, when the people went home and the room was dark and quiet, the library belonged to Sam.

And every night Sam read, and he read, and he read. Sam read picture books and chapter books. He read biographies and poetry, cookbooks and sports books, fairy tales and ghost stories, and mysteries by the dozen.

BASEBALL ALMANAC
2006
796.357 Yuppo
B Einstein
J.A. Gorton
LAOTZU
299.5 Gor
sden
Spooked!
J FIC Mar
VEGETABLES A-Z
I. Alyssum
641.5 Aly
WORLD TALES
398.2 Kahn
RY Creepy and Crawlie
FIC Ave
nd red with white polka dots.
And they lived happily ever after.

Sam's mind was filled with facts and information and images of far-away places, and his imagination brimmed over with wonder and fantasy.

One night Sam decided that it was time he wrote a book of his own!

Sam folded over some little squares of paper he took from the librarian's desk, to make the pages. Then he found a pencil that had rolled underneath a shelf, and he began to write. "Write what you know," Sam had read in a book about writing, so Sam wrote about being a mouse. He drew the pictures for his book by posing in his little mirror and then sketching what he saw.

MAR 2008

Sam worked very, very hard, and finally his first book was done. He called it *Squeak! A Mouse's Life*, and he wrote on the cover, "words and pictures by Sam." He went to the biography/autobiography section of the library, and he tucked his first book onto the shelf. Then he went back to his little hole in the wall and waited.

Ruth
Squeak!
A MOUSE'S LIFE
words and pictures by
Schubert
JB
Schub
Albert Schweitzer
JB
Sch
Sequoyah
JB
Seq
Dr. Seuss
JB
Seu

I ♥ BOOKS
Squeak!
MONK
ON SALE

The next afternoon, sunlight streamed in through the library windows.

"What's this?" asked a girl whose teacher had sent her to the library to do a book report.

"I've never seen anything like this before," said the librarian, and she put *Squeak! A Mouse's Life* on her desk. Later she showed it to the other librarians.

Sam decided to write another book. It was called *The Lonely Cheese*, and working on the book made him feel very hungry. It was a good thing that he always found so many crumbs to eat by the waste basket in the hallway! When he had finished the illustrations, Sam scurried to the picture book section and proudly placed his latest book on the shelf. Then he went back to his little hole in the wall and waited.

THE BIG FALL
by Egbert Shellton
HIPPO
The Lonely Cheese
by
Sam

the
Lonely
Cheese

The next morning, sunlight streamed in through the library windows.

"What's this?" asked a little boy who was looking for a big book about trucks.

"It's another book by Sam," said the librarian. "Just who is this Sam?" she thought to herself, and put *The Lonely Cheese* on her desk.

Later she showed it to the children at story time.

Sam decided to write a chapter book. It was called *The Mystery of Mouse Mansion*, and it gave Sam goose bumps when he wrote down the scary parts. The full moon was shining down through the windows of the darkened library when Sam crept over to the mystery section and sneakily placed his book on the shelf. Then he went back to his little hole in the wall and waited.

DANGER BOY

e Serpent's Secret

HE FEARSOME FAMILY

THE MYSTE
OF
MOUSE MANS

by Sam

J
FIC
Smith

J
FIC
Stamey

The next day, sunlight streamed in through the library windows.

"What's this?" asked a teenager who was looking for a good creepy book to read before bed.

"We've got to find out who this Sam is," said the librarian. "I'll leave a note on the bulletin board and tell him that I would like to meet our new author!" She put *The Mystery of Mouse Mansion* on her desk, and later she showed it to the writing class that came in after school.

That night, Sam found the note. It read:

Dear Sam,

All of us at the library have been enjoying your books immensely. We are all wondering who this mysterious Sam really is! Whoever you are, you certainly have a lot of talent. Not everyone has it in them to write even a single book, let alone three! We think it would be fun to have a "Meet the Author Day," with you as our special guest! The children would love to hear you read your books and share some of your secrets for writing.

Yours truly,

Mrs. Forrester, Head Librarian

ON THE RADIO

Sam felt very nervous. He was happy that the children at the library liked his books. He was flattered that they wanted to meet him. But mice, as a rule, are very shy when it comes to meeting people! Sam could not understand why people thought that writing and making up stories was so hard. If only they would try, they might find out that writing was really lots of fun.

Sam had an idea. He went to the librarian's desk and got some supplies. All night long he wrote and drew and snipped and folded and stapled his little rectangles of paper into mouse-size books.

Meet the Author!

In the morning, when the librarian opened up the children's room, there was a sheet of paper taped to the door. "Meet the author today!" it read. A little girl was the first to see Sam's display, all set up on the front table.

"What is this?" she asked. There sat a tissue box, with a pair of pencils taped to the sides and a banner stretched across the top. On the banner was written, "Meet the Author!" with an arrow pointing down.

t the Auth

The girl bent over to look in the empty tissue box. "Oh!" she said in surprise, for there at the bottom of the box lay Sam's little mirror, and in the mirror the little girl saw her own face smiling up at her. "Me?" she said. "An author?" Next to the mirror was a stack of tiny blank books and a pile of pencils that Sam had sharpened with his little teeth!

Meet the Author!
YELLOW
BE MINE